The Trouble with Babies

The Trouble with Babies

by Martha Freeman

illustrated by
Cat Bowman
Smith

Holiday House/New York

Library of Congress Cataloging-in-Publication Data
Freeman, Martha, 1956–
The trouble with babies / by Martha Freeman ; illustrated by Cat Bowman Smith.—1st ed.
p.   cm.
Prequel: The trouble with cats.
Summary: Nine-year-old Holly tries to adjust to a new home with a neighbor who
has just invented a de-yukkification device.
ISBN 0-8234-1698-4 (hardcover)
[1. Moving, Household—Fiction.   2. Neighbors—Fiction.   3. Stepfathers—Fiction.
4. San Francisco (Calif.)—Fiction.]   I. Smith, Cat Bowman, ill.   II. Title.

PZ7.F87496 Tq 2002
[Fic]—dc21   2001051479

For Jim and Alan,
two great dads

Chapter 1

There was a strange silver something in the back-yard next door. It was the size of a washing machine. It had dials and colored lights and buttons. From each corner dangled tin cans tied to strings.

I was not spying when I looked over the fence and saw it. I was looking for Max Cat.

He had escaped again. Escape is what Max Cat does.

A boy came out of the house next door and walked toward the something. He had curly hair and black eyebrows. He was carrying a cardboard box. It looked heavy. My friend Kimmi would have hollered, "Hello, boy! We just moved into this house today! What are you doing?"

I am not like Kimmi. I ducked so that the boy couldn't see me. I watched him between the slats in the fence. He opened a door in the strange thing and put the heavy box inside. He pulled a notebook out of his pocket and wrote in it. He talked as he wrote. I couldn't hear what he said. Finally, he pressed a button. Something inside the box whirred. The lights blinked on and off.

Uh-oh, I thought. Next door to our new house lives a junior genius. He has invented a time machine. He has kidnapped Max Cat. He is sending Max Cat into the future.

But at that very moment, I heard William holler, *"Here, cat-cat-cat!"*

And I heard my mom say, "There's a tail skittering under the hedge!"

"Holly!" William called to me. "That's your sector! Grab him!"

I turned toward the hedge. Sure enough, here came the tail. I lunged just ahead of it and landed on my tummy. I was not clutching an armful of cat. I was clutching an armful of hedge. Max, meanwhile, shot toward the yard next door. And smacked into the fence.

Our family has four cats. Max is the escape artist. Also the klutz.

I stood up, brushed myself off, and crept toward him. "Poor kitty," I said. "Now hold still. I've got you!"

Max swiped a paw across the bruised place on his head then watched me close in on him. He looked calm. He had seen something I had not. A gap under the fence. Like all cats, Max can be small if he needs to be. At the last possible second, with my fingers grazing his fur, he performed the incredible shrinking-cat trick. In a flash, he was on the other side, loping toward the silver something.

What would junior genius boy do to him? Did he really have a time machine?

"Come back, Max!" I called.

The boy heard me and spotted Max at the same time. He dropped his notebook. "Shoo! Shoo, cat!" He waved and stomped.

Max has too much self-respect to pay attention to such behavior. Ignoring the boy, he nosed around the box. Then he side-rubbed it the way he side-rubs my legs when he's hungry. "Meow?" he asked in his squeaky voice. "Meow?"

"Get away from my device!" the boy hollered at Max. Then he looked up at me. "He's disrupting the experiment!"

"I'm sorry!" I said. "I'll get him. But I have to come around."

At that moment, William appeared at the back door. "Mission accomplished?" he asked me.

"No!" I said. "And now your cat is disrupting the experiment, too!"

It is a funny thing that when one of the cats does something bad, it is William's cat. When it does something good, it is my cat. That's how I see it. William may see it differently. William is my stepfather.

He came down the back steps and stood beside me at the fence. "Greetings, young man," he called over. "Interesting machine, that. Your own invention?"

The young man was upset. But not upset enough to be rude to a grown-up he didn't know. "Yes, it is," he said. "Could you come and get your cat, please?"

"Certainly," said William. "And I apologize for any inconvenience."

William walked away from the fence. I thought he was going around the house to get into the neighbors' yard. But instead he turned back toward me, ran three steps, grabbed the fence, and vaulted over it.

"Wow!" I was impressed. "I didn't know you could do that!"

William is forty-nine years old. He is bald and wears glasses. You don't think of old, bald people with glasses vaulting over fences.

But the boy was not impressed. He was looking at his watch. Now he pressed the button on the silver something again. The whirring stopped. The lights went out. The boy opened the door. He pulled the box out. He looked inside. He grinned.

"It works!" he said. Then he looked up at William. "It's easier to go through the gate."

I looked along the fence. Sure enough, there was a gate near the back corner. It was hard to see because there was ivy over it.

William picked up Max. Max purred. "Now now, Maximilian," William said to his cat. "No more of this behavior. The world is wide and can be wicked."

William's right about that, I thought. You never know when a junior genius might send you to the future.

Chapter 2

After that, William handed Max over the fence to me. And Mom came out to say George had disappeared.

George is another cat. He doesn't escape, and he is not especially a klutz. What he does is he disappears. We always find him. So I wasn't too worried. But then I thought of something. Maybe it was George who had been in junior genius boy's machine. Maybe it was George he had sent to the future.

I was going to ask the boy about this, but he was already carrying the heavy box back to the house. Some water sloshed out of it. That was weird. What did water have to do with a time machine? Did water have anything to do with George?

William was still on the other side of the fence. I remembered his amazing stunt.

"Are you going to do it again?" I asked him. "Show Mom! She'll never believe it! *Please?*"

"What won't I believe?" Mom said.

William shook his head. "Only one matinee performance on Sundays," he said. "I don't want to bore my audience."

Later that night, we found George. Boxes were stacked almost to the ceiling in our new living room. He was asleep on top of the tallest stack. All you could see was the tip of his tail dangling over.

The next morning, I woke up in my new room for the first time. It was Monday. Here in San Francisco, summer mornings have fog. But that day there was none. It was the sun that woke me up. This was *so* not fair. There was no school. I didn't have to be awake at all.

We had moved from a tiny apartment in the Potrero Hill part of San Francisco to this medium-size house in the West Portal part. We needed more room, Mom and William said. I was signed up for soccer camp the next week. But this week I was going to acclimate myself to my new surroundings. That's how William explained it. In other words, this week I had nothing to do except unpack boxes.

I closed my eyes and rolled over. But who could sleep in so much sunlight? I gave up. Boo

Cat was hogging my pillow. I pushed up on one elbow and shoved him off—just in time to spot Wilbur Cat dashing out my door. Hanging from his mouth was a purple polka-dot kneesock.

Oh, shoot! I must have left my suitcase unlatched. Wilbur Cat likes to eat popcorn and chocolate chip cookies. But socks are his favorite.

I was out of bed and after him in a flash. My friend Sylvie had given me those polka-dot socks. She never meant for them to be cat food.

Mom and William were in the kitchen when I ran through. Mom pointed toward the dining room. "He went thataway."

Through the door, I saw Wilbur crouched on the table. He must have thought this was a very good place to eat a kneesock for breakfast. But it was a very bad place to hide. Before he could leap away, I grabbed him. Then I squeezed his cheeks so that his mouth opened. Patiently, tooth by tooth, I removed the sock.

"Oh, Wilbur," I said. "Why couldn't you eat homework or ties or something? Why does it have to be socks?"

Wilbur looked at me. His eyes were not sorry. His eyes were disappointed and hungry. I held the sock up to the light. Only a few holes. I shook it to remove the cat spit. Then I released Wilbur and went into the kitchen to whine to Mom.

Chapter 3

Nothing was normal that day. In my bedroom was all that unnatural sunlight. In the kitchen, both the *San Francisco Chronicle* and the espresso-maker were missing.

William is a creature of habit. So far as I know, there has never been a morning when he didn't read the *San Francisco Chronicle* and drink cappuccino. For cappuccino, you need espresso.

Mom nuked William a cup of instant coffee. William leaned against the counter and leafed through the telephone book. Then he threw that down and paced to the other end of the kitchen. Then he paced back. He sipped his coffee. He frowned. He was driving Mom crazy. She handed him his suit jacket. That was her gentle way to suggest it was time for him to leave.

He understood. "Where's my briefcase?"

"Front seat." She kissed him on the cheek and said, "Knock 'em dead in court today."

William is a boring old lawyer. At night after work, he writes stories that make no sense.

Now he grunted and opened the door that led from the kitchen to the garage. He went down a step. He fumbled on the garage wall for the electric opener. "How does this thing work?" he muttered.

Mom closed the kitchen door before he figured it out. It's possible William spent the whole day trying to get out of the garage.

For a while after that, I sat and watched Mom. She yanked on drawers. She slashed open boxes. She scattered packing peanuts on the floor. I could see it would be a mistake to whine about cat spit on my kneesock, or to ask about breakfast. I wasn't that hungry. What I really wanted was for things to feel normal. But how could I make that happen? I decided unpacking my own boxes might help.

I went back to my room and tore one open. It was full of books. Each book I pulled out seemed like a friend from my normal life. It was the same with the CDs and tapes in the next box. Some were from when I was little, like Raffi and *Peter and the Wolf.* Mom had wanted to sell them in the moving sale. I was glad I said no way.

After the CDs and tapes were on their shelves, I started on clothes. I was putting underwear in my dresser when Mom came in. She looked pale and sweaty and stressed out.

"A person can only ponder possessions for so long, Holly," she said. "I need a break."

"We could go out for breakfast," I said.

"I like the way you think," said Mom.

Chapter 4

Mom and I walked two blocks to a café. The houses we passed were strange colors. Green. Yellow. Blue. Ours fits right in. It is pink. These colors are not normal for houses. They are normal for the mints my great-grandma keeps in a dish on her TV set.

I liked the café, though. It's called Whole Lotta Shakin'. I thought the name was a joke because San Francisco is famous for earthquakes. But it turned out to be a double joke. On the walls inside were posters from *Shake*speare plays. My favorite showed kings and queens and palm trees. It said TWELFTH NIGHT.

"What's that play about?" I asked after Mom and I sat down.

Mom thought for a minute. "A woman dresses up as a man," she said. "The wrong people fall in love. In the end, the right people fall in love. Same as most Shakespeare comedies."

"I thought Shakespeare was all quotations," I said.

"Quotations, too," said Mom. "There's a good one in *Twelfth Night:* 'Some are born brave, some achieve bravery, and others have bravery thrust upon them.'"

I thought about that while I read the menu. I knew I was not born brave. I wondered if I might get bravery some other way.

The waitress came. I ordered a decaf iced coffee and a chocolate roll. I put three packets of sugar in the iced coffee. Mom had a fruit-and-yogurt parfait with herbal tea. I always thought she hated yogurt.

"What do you think the junior genius was doing with his invention?" I asked Mom.

"The who?" she said.

"You know, from yesterday," I said. "The one who lives next door and has the strange silver something. I think it's a time machine. I only hope he doesn't kidnap cats."

"Kidnap cats!" said Mom. "Why would you say that?"

"I don't know," I said. "I guess it's only that nothing in our new neighborhood seems normal. I mean, a boy with black eyebrows and a mysterious invention? A boy who lives"—I paused for dramatic effect—*"right next door?"*

Mom finished her yogurt. Then she sighed and gave me a sympathy look. "It's a lot of changes for a little girl, isn't it?" she said. "William and I getting married last summer. Moving in with him and the cats. Moving again to the pink house."

I didn't want sighs or sympathy. I wanted to talk about the boy who was probably going to kidnap our cats. "I'm not so little," I protested. "William says I'm nine years old and change. And at least I don't have to go to a new school this time."

"It was lucky Market Street School agreed to let you stay," Mom said. "And this is the last change. At least . . ."

I didn't like the way her voice faded. "At least what?"

She smiled. "At least it's the last move."

"Do you promise?" I asked.

"That kind of promise tempts fate," she said.

"What does 'tempt fate' mean?"

"It means it might bring the opposite of what you want," she said.

We walked home. The house where the junior genius cat-kidnapper lived was on the way. When we got near, I saw he was standing on the front porch. At first, I thought he was talking to someone. Then I realized he was alone, talking to his notebook again. Definitely not normal.

"Hello!" Mom waved at him. "We're the new neighbors!"

Why do moms behave this way? I closed my eyes and prayed to disappear. It didn't work. So I peeked out from between my eyelashes. The boy had stopped talking to himself.

"Uh . . . hi," he said.

"I'm Nancy. And this is my daughter, Holly," Mom said.

Kimmi would have marched up and asked, "What's that silver box in your backyard, anyway?" But I am not like Kimmi. I smiled a smile that probably looked sick or scared.

"Uh . . . hi." His vocabulary seemed to have shrunk since yesterday.

"Well," Mom said cheerfully, "nice to meet you. I'm sure we'll see you again."

I wanted to yell at Mom for being so embarrassing. But what was I supposed to say? Don't be friendly? I kept quiet.

A few seconds later, Mom unlocked our new front door.

"Ready, Holly?" Mom said.

I nodded and crouched down. Mom pushed the door open a crack. Out slithered Max. He always waits by the door. He thinks he is a wild jungle beast trapped in the life of an American house cat. He never gives up hope that someone will free him.

"Sorry, Max." I trapped him in my arms. "You have to live in this house now. You'll get used to it. Maybe."

Chapter 5

"Why are you spying on me?" the junior genius asked.

I bet I turned jelly red.

It was five o'clock that afternoon. I had finished most of the unpacking. My room looked nearly normal. Only there were no posters on my walls yet. And I couldn't find my sand dollar collection.

With nothing to do, I had come outside to peek through the fence. When I did, I learned that junior geniuses are creatures of habit, like William. It was the same time as yesterday, and the boy was doing another time travel experiment. Today, his victim was hidden under a blanket.

Of course, when the boy spotted me, I was totally embarrassed. After all, this time I really was spying.

"I am not spying," I said.

"Then what are you doing?"

I thought fast. "Looking for my cat."

Like a magician, the boy pulled the blanket off the thing he was carrying. "Is this he?"

I forgot about being embarrassed. "You give George back this minute! I don't want him disappearing into the future!"

"The future?" the boy said.

"Or the past, either! You give him back!"

"You think this is a time machine?" the boy asked.

"Of course it's a time machine," I said. "I read books. I see movies. I know what time machines look like."

"You read the wrong books and see the wrong movies," said the boy. "This isn't a time machine. It's a de-yuckification device."

"De-yucka what?" I asked. "And give me back my cat!" I added.

"Don't you want him de-yuckified? No offense, but he needs it."

That was a nasty thing to say. The kind of thing a cat-kidnapper would say. George Cat is slightly overweight. Sometimes along with that goes greasy fur and dandruff. The vet explained this. So George, to be honest, is a bit yucky. But what business was that of this boy's? He didn't even know George. George has many very fine qualities.

The boy with black eyebrows opened the door in the silver box. George didn't complain. But I was so upset I didn't know what to do first. Should I scream? Should I call 911?

"I'm warning you," I said. "I'll . . . I'll vault right over this fence!"

"You'll never make it," he said. "You're too short. Go through the gate. It's never locked."

The boy put George into the machine. I ran down to the back corner of the fence. I ripped ivy leaves away from the gate latch.

"The device is harmless," the boy said. "I put my goldfish in yesterday. Today he's swimming laps. Plus he's a lot less yucky."

I tugged the latch and pushed. The gate lurched open. My heart was pounding as I raced to rescue George, trapped in a mad scientist's de-yucka-ma-box.

Chapter 6

There I was, face-to-face with the junior genius cat-kidnapper. But now what was I supposed to do? Punch him? Wrestle him? Trip him? I suddenly wished I hadn't quit karate after the first lesson.

Then I remembered the number one favorite rule of every preschool teacher: "Use your words."

Well, words were all I had. So I said in a firm and confident voice, "Give me my cat."

And what do you know? The preschool teachers were right. Junior genius boy waffled. "Are you sure you don't want him de-yuckified?" he asked me.

"Yes, I'm sure!"

He sighed. "Too bad." He opened the door. He pulled George Cat out of the machine. He handed George Cat to me.

George Cat didn't care that he had been rescued. He seemed to like the machine just fine. In fact, he sniffed and meowed a couple of times. He acted friendly and hungry, same as Max did yesterday.

I was relieved. I held George like a baby and tickled his tummy. George purred and blinked. Cat fur and dandruff floated around us.

"Thank you," I said. "I guess I should go now." But I didn't want to go. I had nothing to do at home except search for my sand dollar collection. I didn't know any kids here yet. Junior genius boy was strange, but he was a kid.

"Okay, go," he said.

"Okay." I turned toward the gate.

"Wait," he said. "What's your name?"

This was a stupid question. Just this morning my mom had told him I was Holly. But I didn't want to insult him. "My name's Holly Garland," I said. "What's yours?"

"Xavier," he said.

"What?"

"X-A-V-I-E-R," he spelled. Then he said it slowly, "Hah-vee-air."

I had never heard of a name that started with X. It fit a junior genius: the mysterious Dr. X.

"Nice to meet you, Xavier." I hoped I pronounced it right.

He didn't say anything, but he smiled. It was a friendly smile. And hadn't he given me George? Maybe he wasn't a cat-kidnapper. I felt brave enough to ask another question. "Why did you invent a de-yucka-ma-box, anyway?"

"For Annie."

He said "Annie" like I was supposed to know who that was. I didn't want to ask a dumb question. So instead I said, "Oh? Is uh . . . she . . . yucky?"

Xavier looked shocked. "Oh, *no!*" he said. "She's not a bit yucky. She's the opposite of yucky. That's why she hates anything that is yucky."

I still didn't know who Annie was. But I had never heard anybody say "yucky" that many times all at once before. It made me want to say it, too: "Yucky, yucky, yucky, yucky."

Xavier nodded. "That's exactly the problem."

I looked at his machine close-up. It was made from two big cardboard boxes stacked on each other and covered with foil. Strings of red and blue Christmas lights hung from it. About fifty tin cans dangled from the corners. Each can had a hole in the bottom; they were strung together like beads.

The door was a flap in the side of the top box. I opened it. Inside was a tiny, battery-powered fan and a mirror. The mirror and fan were attached to opposite sides with twisty ties. The thing being de-yuckified sat between them on the bottom box.

If there was anything I knew about after moving, it was boxes. These didn't look very sturdy. I thought Dr. X should have duct-taped the flaps shut.

"How does it work?" I asked him.

"Light rays change the yucky molecules into dust. Then the fan blows the dust away," he said. "It's my own invention."

"What do the cans do?" I asked.

"Amplify the light rays," he said.

I nodded like this made sense, which it didn't. But I couldn't help saying, "It's only cardboard and foil, though. Really."

Dr. X frowned. I felt bad. Maybe he actually believed his de-yucka-ma-box worked.

But then he faked a snotty accent: "They didn't understand Edison, either. When Edison invented the CD, they called it tinfoil and cardboard."

I might not be a junior genius, but I am not dumb. "Edison didn't invent the CD. Edison invented the lightbulb."

Dr. X shook his head. "Of course he invented the lightbulb. He also invented 1,092 other things. One of them was the first phonograph— in 1887. It's like a CD. You can look it up."

"I will look it up."

As I said before, George is slightly overweight. My arms were tired from holding him. I didn't know what to think of this Xavier–Dr. X person. Maybe he wasn't a genius at all. A genius wouldn't believe in this stupid machine, would he? Besides, he had sounded like a snot just then. But he did have a friendly smile. And he was the only kid around here I had met.

We stood there. George purred. Dr. X adjusted the Christmas lights on the machine. I looked at the mirror and the fan inside. I didn't see how it could hurt anything.

"Maybe it would be okay to de-yuckify George," I said.

Xavier smiled hopefully. "You mean it?"

"He likes you," I said. "There's one thing, though, before I let you."

"Sure. What?" he asked.

"I want to see how your goldfish turned out."

Chapter 7

Xavier was right about the goldfish. Swimming laps in his bowl, he looked perfectly healthy.

"Holly, meet Copernicus," Xavier said. "Copernicus, this is Holly."

Being introduced to a fish made me giggle. "Am I supposed to shake his fin?"

"Wave your hand over the bowl," said Xavier.

I shifted George Cat to my chest and waved.

"He's polite for a goldfish," said Xavier. "He's flipping his tail at you."

Flipping his tail looked the same as swimming laps to me. "Was he yuckier yesterday?" I asked.

"Much," said Xavier. "See how shiny and orange he is now?"

I nodded. George wiggled. Cat fur and dandruff floated everywhere.

"I like your room," I said. "It looks normal. Mine is so spooky and new."

"We've always lived in this house," Xavier said. "We've always lived next to Annie. I would hate to move."

So if Dr. X lived next to Annie, she must live in the green house on the other side. Was she a person? A kid? Xavier's best friend? Or maybe Annie was a dog, and Xavier's parents wouldn't let him have one, so he played with her. The dog I know best is Clyde. He belongs to my friend Sylvie. He is very friendly and he smells bad. He would be good to test the de-yucka-ma-box on, only he is so big he would never fit inside it.

I looked at the posters on Xavier's wall. I recognized Albert Einstein and Thomas Edison. "Who is that guy?" I pointed at a man with long gray hair.

"Leonardo da Vinci," Xavier answered. "One of the great inventors of all time. And that's Sir Isaac Newton."

My chest was not a good place for George. He was mauling me with his paws. My arm muscles hurt. "Do you think I could put him down?" I asked. "Maybe you could close the door. If we don't watch him every minute, he'll disappear."

Xavier closed the door. I set George on the bed. This was a mistake. His whiskers, ears, and tail all twitched at once. He had spotted Copernicus.

I could imagine George's furry cat brain working: Isn't that a fishy? Isn't a fishy delicious? *Must catch fishy!*

"Uh-oh," I said.

"I better—" Xavier reached for George. But George leaped away, first to the pillow, then to the table where the fishbowl sat. Tail swishing, he looked at Copernicus. It was the same way William looks at his favorite food, sushi.

"I'll get him," I said. George's paw was already in the water, splashing after Copernicus. I was afraid the fish might faint from shock. If giant hairy claws were chasing me around a bowl, I'd faint from shock.

"Get him!" said Xavier. But it wasn't so easy. George was right next to a lamp. If I yanked him I'd knock it over, and maybe the fishbowl, too.

"All right, kitty. All right, George. Don't do anything funny." I tried to get my hand on his neck-flab.

Paw still splashing, George backed away from me. I could see that furry cat brain working again: Find your own fishy, Holly! This one's mine!

But George couldn't get hold of Copernicus any better than I could get hold of George. Frustrated, he pulled his paw out of the water and sniffed it. He must have liked the smell because next he took a lick.

Yummy, thought the furry cat brain. Fish soup. He leaned over the fishbowl and sipped. He was dainty and fast, the way cats are.

It was too gross. "Eeeeeeeyew!" I said.

"Not to worry," said Xavier. "The water has been de-yuckified."

Fish soup seemed to satisfy George. With a last sad look at Copernicus, he jumped back onto the bed. I was relieved. It's so embarrassing when your pet massacres the neighbor's pet.

"Let's get him out of here." I scooped up George. We went down the stairs and back outside.

In the yard, Xavier took out his notebook and wrote something. Then he opened the foil-covered door and looked at me. I looked at George.

"Ready?" I said. George blinked. His tummy was full of fish soup. He probably felt sleepy.

"He's ready." I put him in the machine. Xavier closed the door. "Do we say abracadabra or anything?" I asked.

Xavier looked disgusted. "This is *science*, Holly."

"Sorry," I said.

Xavier looked at his watch. "Ten . . . nine . . . eight . . . seven . . . six . . . five . . . four . . . three . . . two . . . one . . . *now!*" He pressed a button. The lights on the outside blinked. The fan on the inside whirred. The whole silver machine vibrated, which made the tin cans rattle. Poor George Cat, I thought. I hope he's not scared.

It didn't seem right to talk while my cat was being de-yuckified. So I waited a few seconds and whispered, "How long does it take?"

"He was pretty yucky," Xavier whispered back.

We waited some more. Finally, Xavier pressed the button and the lights went off. Then he opened the door.

"Uh-oh," he said.

"Uh-oh, *what*?" I looked inside. There was nothing there but the fan and the mirror. George Cat had done what he does best. He had disappeared.

Chapter 8

Xavier spoke to his notebook as he wrote: "This is very interesting."

"What do you mean, 'interesting'?" I was mad and scared. "Your machine vaporized my cat!"

"Maybe he was yucky through and through." Xavier wrote some more. "In that case, the fan would have blown *all* his molecules away."

George is not yucky through and through, I thought. He is a slightly overweight cat with many very fine qualities. William loves him. Mom loves William. *They will kill me!* Why did I let the junior genius cat-kidnapper put George into that machine?

"What did you do with George?!"

Xavier stopped writing. He looked up. "I'm sorry, Holly. I really don't know. This never happened before. Copernicus was right where I left him in his bowl. Wait. . . ." He wrote some letters and numbers. "H_2O—maybe the water buffered the molecular effect. Maybe we should have put George in a fishbowl—"

"I'll put you in a fishbowl if you don't bring back my cat!"

"What I'm trying to explain—" Xavier began, but then he stopped. The de-yucka-ma-box was walking away. We both stared. "That's *very* interesting!" Xavier murmured.

"It is not interesting," I said. "It's George Cat!"

I tilted the machine. There was George, trapped underneath on the grass. He had been pawing the side. That was what made the machine "walk."

Now I understood what had happened. Instead of being de-yuckified, George had dropped between the cardboard flaps and landed on the grass. When his weight was off them, the flaps bounced back. It was a clever trick.

But Xavier didn't appreciate it. And he didn't pay much attention to the miraculous return of George, either. He cared more about his dumb

invention. "Careful!" he told me. "Don't knock it out of balance!"

George came out from under. I straightened the machine up. "It's fine," I said.

"I'm not so sure." Xavier reached inside the door and fiddled with the twisty ties. "The calibrations are very delicate."

It was getting late. Mom would be wondering where I was. I had had enough of Xavier and his calibrations for one day.

"I'm going home." I picked George up. "Maybe I'll see you tomorrow. I'll bring duct tape."

In my own room a few minutes later, I took a good look at George. Pink nose. Pink tongue. Sharp teeth. Freckled ears. Greasy fur. Dandruff.

He didn't look de-yuckified to me.

Mom made an announcement when William got home: "The kitchen is in no condition for cooking," she said. "And neither am I."

We went out for Thai food. I ate clear noodles and peanuts. Later, I asked Mom if I could use the computer.

"Give it a whirl," she said. "I think I got the connections right."

The encyclopedia program came up: another normal thing in an abnormal world. "It works, Mom!" I called.

T-h-o-m-a-s E-d-i-s-o-n, I typed. The article had the same picture as the poster on Xavier's wall. I read it.

Crud. Dr. X, the junior genius, was right. Edison had patented 1,093 inventions. One was the first phonograph, ancestor of the CD. Worse yet, the article said the phonograph recorded sound on a cardboard cylinder covered with tinfoil.

Chapter 9

One normal thing happened the next morning. The *San Francisco Chronicle* arrived on our doorstep. In other news: The espresso-maker remained lost.

"Holly?" William looked over the edge of the sports section. "What are your plans for the day?"

"Find my sand dollar collection," I said.

"Laudable," said William. "But might I also ask you to do something for me?"

"Sure."

"Would you look for the espresso-maker? Another morning of this"—he held up his mug of nuked instant coffee—"and I won't be responsible for my actions."

"I'll look," I said.

After breakfast, Mom announced, "My clients are screaming for their monthlies."

Mom is a bookkeeper. She works at home. A monthly is something she writes for a business owner. It says what happened to the business's money during the last month. I don't see why the owners don't know already what happened to their money. I know what happened to my money: I spent half on chocolate and doughnuts; I saved half for a scooter.

Anyway, I had my own job to do. "My step-father is screaming for his espresso maker," I said.

That morning, I must have opened a thousand boxes. I found half tubes of toothpaste, half bottles of shampoo, and eroded bars of soap.

I found millions of paper clips, safety pins, and pennies.

I found prehistoric magazines and rock 'n' roll records.

Barbie heads and Barbie shoes.

A coffee can full of broken crayons.

And a whole set of dishes with pink roses on them. I took a saucer into Mom's office.

"Those belonged to your grandmother, your father's mother," she said.

"How come you ended up with them?" I asked.

"Spoils of divorce," she said.

"You mean you stole them from Daddy?"

"I thought they were pretty. He didn't want to haul them to L.A. when he moved."

"A lot of them are chipped," I said.

"Sometimes it's hard to get rid of things," Mom said.

By eleven, I was sick of searching. I hadn't found the espresso-maker or my sand dollar collection. But I had found a dozen rolls of duct tape.

"Can I take some over to Dr. X for his machine?" I asked Mom.

"Dr. X?" she said. "Is that what you call that boy next door? Xavier?"

"In my head I do," I said. "Because it's a good name for a mad scientist."

"Whatever he is, he's welcome to the duct tape," she said. "Would he like chipped dishes with roses on them, too?"

"Paper clips maybe." I put a handful in my pocket.

To make myself brave, I thought of Kimmi. I put two rolls of duct tape on my wrist. I marched over to Dr. X's front door. I rang the doorbell.

Chapter 10

I had expected Dr. X to answer the door. Instead, a man opened it. The man had Dr. X's same curly hair, only it was gray and there was less of it. He had the same friendly smile, only it was on a stretched-out, grown-up face.

So much for being brave like Kimmi. I was so surprised, I didn't say anything.

"Hello," he said. "Are you Xavier's new friend?"

"Holly," I blurted out. "Holly from the pink house."

"Holly from the pink house? I love that show! Come on in. Xavier's upstairs. Probably dissecting Copernicus."

The man's eyes crinkled when he talked. He was funny. It was hard to be scared of him.

"Are you his dad?" I asked.

"Nah, his dad was a goldfish, too. . . . Oh, you mean *Xavier's* dad! Yes! Yes, I am. One of them, anyway. My name's Jim."

"Nice to meet you." I held out my hand to shake his.

"Pretty and well mannered, too! You're acing the new-neighbor game, round one. Now, for ten thousand dollars and the spare key under the doormat, how many angels can dance on the head of a pin?"

"Uh . . . depends on the pin?"

" . . . is *right*! Give the little lady a hand, folks! Why, I think I will." He held out his hand. We shook. I giggled. Dr. X's dad was just as weird as Dr. X, only different.

"Oh, good. It's Holly." Dr. X looked at me from the top of the stairs. "I can use your help. Did you bring a calculator?"

"I brought these." I held up my wrist with the silver duct-tape bangles.

"Awfully big for engagement rings," Jim said. "And anyway, aren't you two rushing things a little?"

Dr. X moaned. "Da-a-a-ad, *please*."

"Sorry, sorry—occupational hazard. I can't leave a straight line uncrossed," Jim said.

"Dad writes comedy," Dr. X explained. "You know, for clubs and TV and junk."

"Junk?" Jim said.

"Sometimes," said Dr. X.

"Sometimes," Jim agreed. "But right now there's a big name awaiting big punch lines. Which I'm late delivering. Thanks for ringing the doorbell, Holly. It was a welcome diversion."

"Thank you," I said.

"Whew." Jim was halfway down the hall. He looked over his shoulder at his son. "Where can we get you some manners like hers?"

"Supermarket?" Dr. X tried.

"Supermarket—that's a good one. What aisle? With the mouthwash?" Jim was still talking when he closed his door.

"Your dad talks to himself. Same as you," I told Dr. X.

"I don't talk to myself."

"You talk to your notebook," I said. "It's the same thing."

"Maybe," he said. "But I don't think I'm like him. He makes everything into a joke. I'm more serious. My grandma says I take after Alan."

"Who's Alan?" I asked.

"My other dad."

He must mean stepdad, I thought. Like William. But before I could ask him, he explained. "I have two dads. And no mom. Alan and Jim are partners."

"Oh, now I get it," I said. "You mean they're gay."

Dr. X nodded. "Exactly."

Mom and William have friends who are gay. Some of them have kids. But this was the first time I had met a kid with two dads and no mom.

"Okay." I shrugged.

"You don't think that's weird?" Dr. X asked me.

"It's not usual," I said. "But it's not weird." I reached into my pocket. "I didn't bring a calculator. But I brought paper clips."

"Good," said Dr. X. "We can attach them to the twisty ties. For extra strength. The device needs a tune-up."

"I'll help," I said. "But you have to promise not to vaporize any cats."

We went through the house into the backyard. There was still no fog. The foil and the tin cans glittered in the sunlight.

We tuned it up. That meant:

1. replacing old twisty ties with new twisty ties,
2. anchoring new twisty ties with paper clips,
3. measuring how far the mirror and fan were from the corners of the machine,
4. replacing two burnt-out Christmas bulbs,
5. duct-taping all flaps closed.

When this was done, Dr. X wrote it down in his notebook. "Okay," he said. "Now all we need is a subject to be de-yuckified." He looked at me hopefully. I shook my head. No cats.

"But," I said, "didn't you tell me you invented the machine for, uh, Annie?"

A sad look crossed Dr. X's face. "For Annie," he said.

I still didn't know whether Annie was a dog or a girl or, for that matter, a guinea pig. Mad scientists did experiments on guinea pigs, didn't they? Would Dr. X look sad about a guinea pig? Maybe if the guinea pig had died. The machine looked harmless, but if it was calibrated wrong . . . Could it have killed a guinea pig named Annie?

Anyway, I didn't want to admit I didn't know, so I had to be careful what I said. "Well, uh, in that case, maybe you could, uh, consider Annie."

Dr. X thought for a minute. Then he smiled. "Good idea," he said.

Since I hadn't had an idea at all, I was surprised. "Is it?"

"Sure," he said. "After all, isn't the whole problem the yucky baby?"

I didn't know if the whole problem was the yucky baby. I didn't know the yucky baby at all. But it sounded like I was supposed to. So what I said was, "The yucky baby."

"Exactly," said Dr. X. "So when are you going to talk to her?"

"To Annie?" I asked. "Or to the yucky baby?"

"Well, to Annie, of course. Babies can't understand English."

"Right," I said. "Obviously."

"Obviously."

"But why do I have to talk to Annie?" I asked.

"Because I can't," he said.

"Oh," I said. Should I ask him why not? Or was I supposed to know that, too? My head was dangerously near dizzy. I tried to put together what I knew so far. Annie must be a person because Dr. X wanted me to talk to her. Even a mad scientist wouldn't expect me to talk to a guinea pig. And

Annie probably had a baby in her family. And something about Annie made Dr. X sad.

It still didn't add up to anything sensible. But I didn't want to disappoint him. He was still the only kid in the neighborhood I knew. So I said, "Well, okay, I guess. I will go talk to her."

"Thanks, Holly!" said Dr. X. And he gave me a big hug.

Chapter 11

I didn't know who Annie was. I didn't know who the yucky baby was. I didn't know how I was going to find out. Let alone go and talk to them about Dr. X's de-yucka-ma-box.

But sometimes you get lucky.

At home, I found Mom on her hands and knees peering under the sofa. This could only mean one thing: cat crisis.

"Which one is it?" I asked her.

"Max," Mom said. "I just finished the count, and he's missing. Could you have let him out?"

The count is a chart on the refrigerator with the name of each cat. Once a day somebody counts them and somebody checks them off.

William doesn't want to lose a single one. They were his whole family before he got Mom and me.

Was it possible Max had sneaked by me when I left for Dr. X's house? It seemed like the cats were getting out a lot lately. I wondered how. "Don't panic, Mom," I said. "I'll go outside and look."

I searched around the front of the house. I crawled down the driveway and looked under the hedge. No skittering tails. No stray paws or noses. I was going to the backyard when my good luck came down the sidewalk. It was a woman walking with one of those baby carriers on her tummy. There was a lump in it. Pink booties stuck out the bottom.

I remembered Dr. X's yucky baby. Was it possible that this was it?

"Hello!" the woman called. "Did you just move in? Welcome to the neighborhood!"

I guess it's a mother thing. First my mother was all friendly with Dr. X. Now this lady was all friendly with me.

I didn't want to sound as dumb as Dr. X had sounded. I wanted to win round two of the new-neighbor game. I took a deep breath. I thought of

Kimmi. I said: "My name is Holly Garland. It's nice to meet you. Is this the yucky baby?"

I didn't really say that last part out loud, did I? That "yucky baby" part?

Yes, I did.

The woman looked as surprised as I felt.

"I didn't mean that." My face turned jelly red. "I mean, I did mean that I'm Holly Garland. That part is the part I meant. . . ."

I wished the woman would smile. But she only looked confused.

"But your yucky baby . . . that part I didn't mean. Except for the baby part. For sure, it's a baby. At least I think so. . . ."

Every syllable made things worse. What did I do? I kept talking.

"In the carrier it's more a lump with pink booties. But I'm sure it's not yucky. Except probably the diapers are yucky. But who can blame it for having yucky diapers? It's a baby. Isn't it?"

Finally I had enough sense to shut up. For a second, no one said anything. Then the woman asked, "Have you been talking to Annie? She's my older daughter. She calls this little one 'yucky baby,' too."

Aha! Annie *was* a person! And this woman, who looked pretty normal except for a little bit confused, must be her mom. And in the carrier was Annie's little sister, kicking her pink booties. Kicking, probably, because she was insulted about being called yucky.

One mystery solved. But there were plenty more. What was Annie like? Why had Dr. X built a de-yucka-ma-box for her? Why couldn't he go talk to her himself?

"I haven't met Annie," I said. "I know about her, though. From Dr. X. I mean from Xavier. I met Xavier."

Now, thank goodness, the woman smiled. "Xavier's a great kid. So bright." She seemed willing to forgive me for calling her baby yucky so long as I was a friend of Xavier's. "I'm Aileen Cohen-Liu. What were you doing out here, Holly? Looking for something?"

"Max," I said. "He's the one that escapes."

Aileen Cohen-Liu was not following the conversation too well. It's probably hard to concentrate when you have a tiny baby. "The one what?" she asked.

"The one cat," I said patiently. Then I was so relieved she wasn't mad that I explained all about

George, Boo, and Wilbur, too. And I explained about moving from Potrero Hill. And I started to explain about William and Dr. X both being creatures of habit. But Mom and Max came out on the front porch before I was finished.

"Hello!" Annie's mom called to her. "I'm Aileen. Green house. Is that Max, Boo, George, or Wilbur?"

"I see Holly's filled you in," Mom said. "This is Max. And I'm Nancy Spencer."

"Where was he?" I asked.

"Stuck in the shower. Don't ask me how. I only found him when he started singing," Mom said.

The booties kept kicking. And then came fussing from the lump that was attached. From her pocket, Aileen Cohen-Liu pulled out a pink Binky. She leaned forward so that she could see the baby's face. Then she popped the Binky into the baby's mouth. The mouth sucked hungrily. The fussing stopped.

"That should hold her for a minute," she said. "Now, would either of you care to come over for a cup of tea? I know Annie would like to meet Holly. She's been a little lonely lately."

"That's so nice of you," Mom said. "I wish I could, but I've still got work to do."

"Won't you come and visit, Holly?" Aileen asked.

An invitation to tea sounded like something for a princess. But I was nervous to go without Mom. I wondered if this was what it was like to have bravery thrust upon you.

"Go ahead, sweetie," said Mom. "Get to know the neighbors."

Kimmi would have been proud. "All right," I said, "I will."

Chapter 12

As soon as I saw Annie, I hated her.

She was a regular girl. Nine years old like me. Small. She was wearing an expensive brand of T-shirt and an expensive brand of jeans. Her black hair was French-braided and clipped with a barrette the same color as her T-shirt.

Dr. X was right about one thing. She was the opposite of yucky. She was so neat that I worried my chin might be smeared with jam from breakfast. I wiped it on my sleeve just in case.

Then Annie smiled. It was a bright smile. I decided to give her a second chance. Maybe it wasn't her fault she was perfect.

"I was going to come over and meet you," she said, "but I felt shy, you know? I'm glad Mom dragged you here. I hope you didn't mind too much. Sometimes moms can be bullies, you know?"

We were in Annie's kitchen. Annie's mom had gone upstairs "to deal with the baby," she said. Annie poured hot water into a teapot. The teapot was on a shiny black tray with the teacups and saucers. There was a sugar bowl and a tiny pitcher. It was all as neat as Annie herself.

"Your mom didn't have to drag me," I said. "I wanted to meet you, too." Was this when I should tell her about the de-yucka-ma-box? I didn't feel ready.

"I'll get the sugar cubes," Annie said. "There's milk in the refrigerator. Do you mind pouring it into the pitcher?"

I was so afraid I'd spill that my hand shook. Two drops fell on the tray. I dabbed them with a napkin before Annie noticed. I was very glad she didn't ask me to carry the tray into the dining room.

Annie's grandmother sat at the head of the table. She was soft and round looking. She wore a pale blue sweat suit with pink roses. Her hair looked like a puff of gold cotton candy. "Who's this one?" She looked at me. "Am I supposed to know this one?"

"No, Grandmother, you haven't met her. This is the new neighbor," Annie said. "Holly, this is my grandmother, Mrs. Cohen. Grandmother, this is Holly."

I had never had so much politeness practice in one day. "Nice to meet you, Mrs. Cohen."

"And where did you come from?" Mrs. Cohen asked.

I didn't know what she meant. Should I say the pink house down the street? The stork brought me? "I was born right here in San Francisco," I tried.

This was the wrong answer. "I meant, where did your family come from? Your parents? Your grandparents?"

I wanted to tell Mrs. Cohen what she wanted to know. But I didn't understand exactly what that was. Annie tried to help me. "My mom and my grandmother are Jewish," she said. "Grandmother Cohen's mother came from Poland. My dad was born in China."

"Oh," I said. "Well, we're not Jewish. Or Chinese, either. On Sunday mornings, my mom goes to the Unitarian church. And William—that's my stepfather—he does the crossword puzzle."

Mrs. Cohen nodded. So I kept talking: "Uh . . . my mom was born in San Francisco. And William was born in New York. Some of my grandparents live in Arizona. But they weren't born there, I don't think. And . . . uh, my dad lives in Los Angeles."

"Los Angeles!" Mrs. Cohen shook her head.

"Is that bad?" I asked.

"To each his own." She took a sip of tea and made a face. "Where's the sugar, Annie? When you're old, you need sugar. Without it, you turn bitter."

"You drank your tea before I had a chance to put sugar in it," Annie said.

"You gave the tea to me before it was ready," Mrs. Cohen said.

Annie took her grandmother's teacup and stirred two cubes of sugar into it. "Now drink it up, Grandmother. You don't like it if it isn't hot."

Mrs. Cohen looked at me. "Annie takes care of me like I was a baby," she said. "She should treat her little sister so well."

"The baby is yucky," said Annie. "You are not."

Mrs. Cohen took a sip of her tea and frowned. "It's cold," she said. "I hate cold tea."

"What did I tell you? I'll put it in the microwave, Grandmother. But then drink it right up!"

Annie took the teacup and went into the kitchen. Mrs. Cohen winked at me. I like her, I thought, even if she does order Annie around. My grandparents live far away. I don't see them much.

Annie's mom came down the steps with the baby. "Is the tea ready?" she asked.

"Beyond ready," Mrs. Cohen said. "It's cold."

I took a sip. It was plenty hot for me. Peppermint. "May I see the baby?" I asked.

"Sure. She's clean and ready for company. Here."

I hadn't meant I wanted to hold the baby. I had never held a baby before. But Annie's mother was fast. Before I could argue, she reached over my head and lowered the baby into my lap.

The baby was small and floppy. Her head was flat in back and pointy on top. Was that normal?

I put one hand on each side of her chest to steady her. Even so, I was sure her head would tip sideways, her neck would break, and she would be damaged for life.

Her mom didn't seem worried, though. She sat down across from me and sipped her tea.

I was scared noise might knock the baby over. So I whispered, "How old is she?"

"Why are you whispering?" Mrs. Cohen shouted.

The baby did not fall over. I said, "I don't want to disturb her."

"Ha! Disturb that one? She would sleep through an earthquake. Best baby I ever saw."

"You're her grandmother," Aileen said. "Of course you think she's the best."

"I'm her sister's grandmother, too. And she was a *terrible* baby. Kvetch, kvetch, kvetch—all the time."

"I heard that!" Annie gave the steaming tea to her grandmother.

"You're quite a decent nine-year-old, though," said Aileen. "Come here and I'll give you a kiss. I don't think I've given you a kiss all day."

Annie shook her head. "I am too old for kisses."

"Oh, that's right," said Aileen. "I guess I forgot."

Annie ignored her and frowned at the baby. "Watch out," she told me. "She'll spit up all over you. Or worse."

"Now don't start," said Aileen. "There's not much a baby can do that a damp cloth won't fix. To answer your question, Holly, she is a month old tomorrow." Then she seemed to read my mind. "She'll be prettier in a couple of weeks. Sometimes being born beats them up a little."

The baby did look funny, with her lumpy head and scrunched face. But I liked the way she felt: warm, wriggly, and alive. I like my cats, too, but this was different. The cats are heavier and lazier; their fur gets everywhere; you have to worry about a stray claw poking you.

I didn't think before I said it. It just popped out: "I don't think she's yucky."

Annie frowned. Her mom smiled. Mrs. Cohen laughed. Now I was in an impossible fix. Annie was mad, but I couldn't say sorry without offending her mom.

The baby saved me. Unfortunately, she saved me by burping a stream of white goo into my lap.

Annie grinned. "See?"

Chapter 13

Aileen wiped off the goo with a damp cloth. Then Annie showed me her room. Of course it was as neat as she was. The posters on her wall had nice frames; the pillows matched the bedspread. We talked about starting fourth grade in a couple of weeks. Annie went to a private school. I'd be going back to my old school, Market Street. It's across town. William's going to drive me. Annie told me she goes to gymnastics. I told her about soccer.

But all the time we talked, I was thinking how to tell her about the de-yucka-ma-box.

I was ready to give up when Annie said, "*Eeeyew.* No offense, Holly. But I just got a whiff of baby yuck. You'd better change when you get home."

"Sorry," I said.

"It's not your fault," she said. "You were being nice to hold her, you know? I never hold her if I can help it. She always does that. My grandmother says she's perfect. But really, she's yucky."

I saw my chance. "You hate things that are yucky, don't you?"

"Who doesn't?" Annie asked.

I took a breath and thought of Kimmi. "Did you know there's an invention that makes yucky things not yucky?"

"Huh?"

I wanted to get the brave part over with. "Xavier— You know Xavier. Only I call him Dr. X. Anyway, Xavier. He invented something. A de-yucka-ma-box. Maybe you saw it? It's in his yard. It's silver. It's weird.

"You put something in it. And the something isn't yucky anymore. The fan blows the yuck away. Just like Thomas Edison. At least, that's how he explained it. Dr. X explained it. Not Thomas Edison . . ."

Annie stared at me. I took another breath. "It

worked great on Copernicus," I said. "You should see how shiny and orange he is. I don't think it worked on George Cat. But he got vaporized, so it wasn't a fair test. And anyway, he always disappears. Which isn't Dr. X's fault. I mean, Xavier's fault.

"But he invented it for you. Because he knows you hate yuck. It was sweet of him, I think. Don't you think?"

I knew I had done a bad job explaining. I was terrified that Annie would want me to start over. I wasn't brave enough to do that. I wasn't smart enough to do that. But Annie surprised me.

"I get it." She nodded. "He invented this de-yucka-ma-box for me. And you're right—it was sweet. But don't you get it? It was *too* sweet. That's the whole problem."

I didn't understand. "What do you mean?"

"It's hard to explain," she said. "But he has a *crush* on me. It's awful. We used to be regular friends, but now we can't be anymore because of this stupid crush. He is always doing extra-nice things, you know? Complimenting me. Giving me stuff. It's, I don't know, too much somehow. Has anybody ever had a crush on you?"

I shook my head. I couldn't even imagine.

"Nobody ever had a crush on me, either, till Xavier," she said. "And it's terrible! Whenever he looks at me it's like . . ."

"Like what?" I asked.

"I don't want to sound stuck-up. But like I'm a star on MTV or something. And he treats me the same way. You can't talk to a person like that, you know?"

I thought about the dreamy way Xavier had called Annie "the opposite of yucky." Maybe that was what she meant. "But you used to be friends," I said.

"That's the worst part! We used to have fun together. We used to talk about all sorts of things. We used to do homework sometimes. But then it all changed. And you know what else?"

"What else?" I asked.

"Everything I say hurts his feelings. Like once we were doing arithmetic. And he got a problem wrong. And I told him the right answer. And it was like he was going to cry!" She rolled her eyes.

I shook my head. "It does sound terrible," I said. "I hope nobody ever gets a crush on me."

"I hope not, too," said Annie.

By then it was getting late. "I better go," I said.

"I'm glad you came over," said Annie. "I'm glad you told me about the de-yuck invention. And you know what? Even though it means I'll have to see Xavier, I think maybe it's worth a try."

Now I was confused. "What's worth a try?"

"His invention. Maybe it works. Tell him I'll bring the yucky baby over tomorrow."

Chapter 14

"Now what do we do?" I asked.

I was talking to Dr. X on the phone. It was the same night. We had just come back from dinner at the taqueria.

"You mean Annie's really coming here? Tomorrow?" Dr. X was thrilled.

I tried to be patient. "I told you already. Annie is coming there tomorrow. But what do we do?"

"She doesn't hate me anymore?"

"She didn't say if she hates you. She only said she wants to put the baby in the machine. And now I am asking you again: *What do we do?*"

"We put the baby in the machine," Dr. X said. "I mean, in the de-yuckification device. It's what

Annie wants." Even over the phone, I could tell what Annie had been talking about. His voice had gone all daydreamy.

"But we can't!" I said. "Anyway, it's too small for a baby. Isn't it?"

"Nope," said Dr. X. "The baby will just fit. I measured."

Suddenly, I realized something. "Wait a minute, Dr. X. Was this your plan all along? To put Annie's baby in the machine?"

"Dr. X?" he repeated. "Since when am I Dr. X?"

I had called him that in my head so much I forgot he didn't know. I didn't want to say it was a good name for a mad scientist. So I only said it was a good nickname.

"Dr. X," he said. "Dr. X. You know what? I like it. I never had a nickname before."

"Well, you've got one now. And don't change the subject," I said. "Were you planning all along to put the baby in the machine?"

"Why not?"

"Why not?" I couldn't believe it. "Because . . . Because . . . Well, for one thing, it vaporized George Cat!"

There was a pause. Dr. X must have been thinking. "We've tuned it since then," he said.

"Besides, it didn't really vaporize George Cat. He fell through to the bottom. He was fine."

"He was fine," I said, "because cats land on their feet. But babies land on their heads! Get it?"

"You're forgetting the duct tape," he said.

We argued some more. We didn't agree about putting the baby in the machine. But we did agree to meet Annie and the baby in Dr. X's backyard.

"Let me call her." Dr. X sounded really excited. "Okay? I'll tell her five o'clock. Okay?"

"Five o'clock," I said. It was after I hung up that I remembered about five o'clock. That was when the junior genius—creature of habit— always did his experiments.

Later that night, the phone rang.

"For you, Holly!" Mom called. I went to pick up my phone. Boo was asleep on top of it. I shoved him onto the floor. He jumped into my lap. I let him stay.

"Camp was great!" Kimmi told me. "I met all these cool kids; I didn't have to water a single begonia."

Kimmi's stepfather raises begonias. Kimmi's job is to water them. She says she hates it. But I

don't think she hates it as much as she likes saying she hates it.

I told her about Dr. X and his machine, and George being vaporized, and Annie, who hates Dr. X, and the yucky baby.

"They were best friends," I explained. "But then a disaster happened. He got a crush on her. When she found out, she started hating him. Isn't that sad?"

"Boys don't get crushes," Kimmi said. "They play baseball."

"Dr. X doesn't," I said. "He's a junior genius."

"If you say so," Kimmi said. "But there's still one thing I don't get. Why does Annie mind so much about yucky things?"

"Dr. X thinks it started with diapers."

"Annie wears diapers?!" Kimmi said.

"Kimmi, are you paying attention? Annie is a grown-up kid like us! It's the new baby that wears diapers. Also, she drools and spits up. Annie thinks the baby's yucky."

"Awwwwwww, I *love* babies! They aren't yucky; they're *cute*," Kimmi said.

"I think so, too." I thought of how Annie's sister had felt when she was in my lap—before she spit white goo, at least. "And tomorrow they're going to put her in the machine."

"They can't do that!" Kimmi said. "She's a person, not an experiment."

"That's what I think!" I said. "But everybody else wants to try. And I'm not brave enough to stop them. Can you come over? You're brave. You could stop them."

"I can't tomorrow, Holly," Kimmi said. "Mom missed me when I was at camp. She wants me to stay home for a while. She'll get sick of me soon, though. Then I'll come."

Chapter 15

The next morning I felt bad I hadn't found the espresso-maker for William. So I took money from my scooter savings and walked to the café.

It was sunny again. Blue sky was getting on my nerves.

The guy working behind the counter was tall and skinny. His head was shaved. There was a ring in his left eyebrow. There was a dragonfly tattooed on his cheek.

I liked him instantly.

"One mocha, one cappuccino, please," I said. I would have ordered something for Mom, too, but she said she was "off coffee."

"So much caffeine, so little time," the guy answered. "Singles or doubles?"

"Single mocha. Double cappuccino," I said. "The cappuccino is for William."

The guy spun around and did dance steps. "Whatever William wants, William gets . . . ," he sang. The machine hissed. The guy mixed everything up. He spun around again and placed the cups in front of me. "Voilà!"

I put the money on the counter. "Thank you. I liked your song."

"Come back tomorrow," he said. "I tell jokes."

At home, I handed William the cappuccino. He took a sip. "Aaaah!" He closed his eyes. "Nectar of the gods. God bless you, Holly."

Mom kissed the top of my head.

I thought about Annie's saying she was too old for kisses from her mom. I liked them okay— unless I was mad about something. Was Annie mad at her mom? Was it because of the new baby?

I didn't want to spend the day worrying about the experiment. So I decided to make one more search among the boxes. Probably we had goofed and sold the espresso-maker for a dime at our

moving sale. Probably my sand dollar collection was on a shelf at the Salvation Army store. Still, it was worth a try.

I opened several boring boxes. Inside one were file folders stuffed with stories William had written. I pulled one story out. It was called "Abnormal." I read a little:

> Lily disliked the excitement and drama brought by so many changes in her life. How she longed for a settled contentment! For the succor of real friends! For the cocoon of familiar surroundings! Alas, our heroine failed to realize that the key to contentment lay within herself. In time she would turn introspective. . . .

I sighed. Long words. No sense. I will never understand the stuff William writes. Not if I live to be forty-nine years old.

I put the folder back in its box. In our old apartment, William had kept his stories in a file cabinet in the laundry room. Here there would be space for them in Mom's office. I carried the box in and dropped it—thump—on the floor. At the computer, Mom jumped.

"Sorry," I said. "It's heavy. Can we go out to lunch? Yesterday I had cookies. It wasn't very healthy."

"Oh, sweetie, I wish we could." Mom swiveled her chair to look at me. "There's something I want to talk to you about, too. But I'm still up to my eyeballs. Would tomorrow be okay? For now, there's brie in the fridge. And William picked up a box of water crackers. Add some grapes, and it's a balanced meal."

Mom swiveled back. On her computer screen was a lot of arithmetic. I was hungry. But grateful to be a kid.

I ate the crackers in the living room while I opened the last three moving boxes. There was nothing good in the first one. In the second one was Boo Cat, asleep on a stack of place mats. How did he get there? That's one of the mysteries of Boo Cat.

The last box. It felt like that last Christmas present. I lifted it. I shook it. I drummed on it. I tore the cardboard open.

"Hooray!"

Inside was the espresso-maker. When I saw it, some corner of memory made me look in the pot, too. There was my sand dollar collection. A couple were broken. I guess I shouldn't have shaken the box.

I ran to tell Mom.

"The heavens rejoice!" she said. "But whoever packed that box? What an odd combination of items."

I looked at my shoes. "I think maybe I packed it."

"You're kidding! And you didn't remember? Why not?"

I didn't know why not. Too many boxes, I guess. But then I thought of something we learned in school last year. "Malnutrition," I said. It meant you had enough to eat but not enough that was healthy. "The school nurse says you can't think right if you have malnutrition."

Mom laughed. "Tomorrow, Holly. I promise. We'll go out to lunch. And we'll eat properly."

Chapter 16

At 4:59 I opened the back door a crack, blocked Max with my foot, and slipped through. Between the slats in the fence, I saw Dr. X and Annie. Did she have the baby with her? I couldn't see.

During the afternoon I had arranged my sand dollar collection. Then I called Sylvie. Her family was back from vacation. They had gone to a dude ranch. They even took their big smelly dog, Clyde.

I told Sylvie about the experiment. She said I was worrying too much. Sylvie usually thinks I am worrying too much.

"I've been around babies plenty," Sylvie said. "When they're not happy, they scream. Screaming is the baby alarm system. If the alarm goes off, you pick the baby up and give it a Binky. This shuts off the alarm. It's simple. Just make sure Annie has a Binky with her."

I thought of Sylvie as I pushed away ivy leaves and opened the gate. Was I worrying too much? Maybe Kimmi was wrong. Maybe I should stop worrying. Besides, I was curious. Would the de-yucka-ma-box really work? Would it stop white-goo attacks? What did a de-yuckified baby look like?

Now Annie turned to face me. The baby was in her arms. She was asleep as usual, wrapped in a blanket. "Your mom let you bring her?" I asked.

"My grandmother was baby-sitting," she said. "I told her I was taking her out in the backyard. I didn't say whose backyard. Grandmother believes babies need fresh air."

"Did you bring a Binky?" I asked.

"Right here." Annie pulled it out from the folds of the blanket.

I looked down at the baby. Asleep, her face was less scrunched. She was almost pretty. I didn't want anything bad to happen to her.

Dr. X hadn't said anything. Now I saw he was looking at Annie. His expression was dopey. Meanwhile, Annie aimed her eyes everywhere except at him.

"Yoo-hoo?" I said. "Dr. X? Earth to junior genius?"

"Huh?" Dr. X answered me, but he kept looking at Annie.

Finally, she couldn't stand it. "Xavier—would you *please* stop staring!"

Dr. X reacted like he'd been bee stung. "What?"

"It is so totally yucky," she said. "You know?"

"I'm really sorry," Dr. X said. "I'll never do it again. Never. I mean, I wouldn't ever do anything to bug you or annoy you or even irritate you the tiniest—"

"I know, Xavier," Annie interrupted. "I really know. And I appreciate that you made the machine for me, too. I bet it was a lot of work. So now let's try it out. Okay?"

Dr. X's face lit up. "Okay!" he said. "Everything's ready. I checked the tape. The twisty ties are triple twisted."

"I still don't think this is a good idea," I said.

"I keep telling you, there's nothing to worry about," said Dr. X. "Remember Copernicus."

I crossed my arms. "Are we going to put the baby in a fishbowl, too?"

"Fishbowl?" Annie said.

Dr. X frowned at me. "Holly's making a joke. I used to think maybe the water in Copernicus's bowl buffered the light rays. But now I'm sure it's safe. The baby will be fine."

A worry shadow crossed Annie's face. "As long as you're sure," she said. "My parents would kill me if anything happened to her."

"Perfectly safe," Dr. X said.

"Okay," Annie said. "So what do we do next? How does it work?"

Dr. X explained. It still sounded incredible. The yucky molecules turn to dust and blow away? And George was as yucky as ever. But he wasn't in the machine very long. And I remembered the encyclopedia entry on Edison's sound recording. Cardboard and tinfoil, just like the de-yucka-ma-box.

"Okay, are we ready?" Dr. X gave Annie another dopey look. If this was a cartoon, I thought, cupids would be flying around his head. "You open the door and put the yucky baby in," he said. "I'll close the door and throw the switch. She won't be yucky when she comes out."

Annie nodded and took a step toward the machine. She looked at the door in the side. She frowned. She held on to the baby.

"Everything's ready," Dr. X said. "As soon as she's in the machine, we'll begin the countdown. Go ahead, Annie."

Annie nodded again. But she kept frowning. And she didn't move.

"I'll put her in if you don't want to." Dr. X reached for the baby in Annie's arms.

At the same time, the baby sneezed. Baby snot sprayed everywhere.

Dr. X yanked his hands away and wiped them on his jeans. "Gross!" he said.

I couldn't help it. I giggled. The baby grunted, "Eh-ch-eh." Then she opened her eyes and kicked at her blanket.

Annie smiled at the wide-eyed, scrunchy face. "Don't call her gross," she said.

"Oh, sorry," said Dr. X. "I didn't mean . . . But hey, wait a minute. You're the one who says she's yucky."

"Yucky isn't the same as gross."

This was weird. It seemed like suddenly Annie liked the baby.

"Sorry, Annie. Technically speaking, you're right," said Dr. X. "Yucky isn't gross. Now, let us proceed. Would you like to put the baby in the

machine? Or shall I? After that sneeze, she *really* needs to be de-yuckified."

Annie looked up. "I've changed my mind," she said. "You know?"

I couldn't believe it. I thought Annie was so positive. It had been her idea.

Dr. X looked surprised; then he looked heartbroken. "But why?" he asked.

"I don't know. I just know it's not right. Especially now that she's awake. What if she got lonely in there? After all—she's my sister."

It was an afternoon of miracles. Annie had called the yucky baby her sister. And then she did something else amazing: She kissed the yucky baby—right on her snotty nose.

The kiss must have been a cue. Because right after, it all got crazy.

Chapter 17

The first part seemed innocent enough. It was only a soft sound. A very familiar soft sound: "Meow?"

What was strange was that the sound had come from inside the machine. Dr. X and Annie and I looked at one another. I shrugged. Slowly, carefully, Dr. X pulled open the door. A paw poked through the narrow opening. Then a nose. Then all of Boo Cat himself.

How did he get in there?

Why did he get in there?

More mysteries of Boo Cat.

But one thing was sure. He really wanted out. Because as soon as the gap was wide enough, he came at us like a flying squirrel.

And at the same moment, a man came running down the back steps of Dr. X's house. He was so upset he tugged at the hair on his head. "Oh my gosh, oh my gosh!" the man cried. "That animal's attacking Aileen's baby!"

Dr. X shook his head. "That's Alan," he said. "So much for science."

Actually, Boo was not attacking the baby. The baby just happened to be in Boo's flight path. Luckily, Annie had seen the cat coming and pivoted. Meanwhile, I had dived to intercept him— too late. *Oooooooof*—I hit the grass stomach first. Just as I did, a shadow flew over.

"It's a bird! It's a plane!" Jim yelled from the window. But it was really William, vaulting the fence and charging across the yard, inches behind Boo.

"Wow! For an old guy—" Annie started to say, but she never finished her sentence because right behind Alan appeared Mrs. Cohen.

"This is giving the baby fresh air? You brought her practically to a different zip code!" Mrs. Cohen was breathing hard. Her words came out in gasps. "I looked in the back yard, I looked in the front yard. When your mother finds out—"

But that sentence never was finished, either. Jim came out of the house next. He didn't look upset. He just looked puzzled.

"So I'm sitting in my office and this blur stomps through like a baby elephant, and— Oh, hi, Mrs. Cohen. I guess that was you. And then I see Superman there— What's the matter, Alan? I didn't know you were home. Hi, kids. Nothing's wrong, I trust."

"I'll tell you what's wrong," Alan said. "Your son here was just about to experiment on a live human being!"

"My son? As opposed to, let us say, *your* son?" Jim asked.

"All right, *our* son."

"Surely you jest," said Jim. No one answered. "Or surely you don't. Well, Xavier, would you like to explain yourself?"

But Xavier did not like. Xavier was too disgusted. When Annie changed her mind, he lost his chance for love and his chance for scientific glory. That was a lot to lose, I guess. Instead of answering, he sighed. Then he walked around Mrs. Cohen, and up the steps, and into the house.

Annie watched him go. "I think he might be upset, you know?"

"Not as upset as your mama will be," said Mrs. Cohen. "Now hand me that baby. We're going home!"

The baby had fallen back to sleep. Annie did not give her to Mrs. Cohen. She held her close. "Come on, Laura," she said. "I'm not sure, but I think you and I are in trouble."

Mrs. Cohen looked at me with wide eyes. "Laura?" she repeated. "*Oy vey!* I was just getting used to 'yucky baby'!"

Chapter 18

Of all the cats, Wilbur is easiest to find. You look for an open sock drawer, and there he is, chowing down. Boo is next easiest. You look where you don't want him to be. Like on your pillow. Or shedding on the place mats. Or asleep on top of the phone when your friend calls.

I was explaining this to William. We were in the bathroom. He was sitting on the counter, poking his palm with a pair of tweezers. He was trying to remove a splinter. He had gotten it from the fence.

"So to find Boo now we just think where we don't want him to be," I said.

"Hmmmm," said William.

"Where did you last see him?" I asked.

"Vanished behind the Cohen-Lius' house—*ow!*" William had jabbed himself with the tweezers.

"Do you want me to try?" Mom was standing in the doorway.

"No, I do not want you to try." William jabbed again. "Ow! There. Got it." He held the splinter up like a prize fish. It was microscopic.

Mom nodded. "Big one," she said. "I'll get antiseptic."

"I don't *want* antiseptic," said William.

"Yes, you do," said Mom. "Hold still."

Mom dabbed his hand with red stuff. William made owie faces. "What baffles me," he said, "is how the cats keep getting out."

I felt bad for him. "Don't worry, William," I said. "I will find Boo."

And I did.

I called Annie and told her Boo was still missing. "Could you check in the yucky baby's room?"

"Her name is Laura," Annie said.

"Sorry," I said. "Could you check in Laura's room?"

"No problem," said Annie. "I'll call you back."

Instead of calling, Annie showed up at the front door. Boo Cat was in her arms.

"I didn't even have to check," she said. "The second I hung up, I heard this hysterical shrieking."

"Uh-oh," I said.

"No, it's okay. It wasn't Laura," Annie said. "It was Grandmother. She was going to put Laura down to sleep. She turned back the blanket in the bassinet—"

"—and there was Boo Cat." I finished her sentence.

"Exactly," said Annie. "Grandmother has a thing about cats and babies. She thinks cats are bad luck or something. So she got hysterical."

"You're not bad luck, are you, Boo?" I took him from Annie. "William will be so happy. I bet

he lets Boo sleep on his pillow tonight. Do you want to come in?" I asked Annie.

"I can't."

"Are you grounded? Are you in trouble?"

"Are you kidding?" Annie said. "Mom was so ecstatic that I called the baby Laura. I'm going home to ask her to double my allowance. But can I ask you something first?"

"Sure."

"How did you know your cat was in Laura's room?"

"I'm not sure exactly," I said. "I think it's being around them a lot. You can't help it. You pick up cat sense."

Chapter 19

The next morning, the fog rolled in.

William, Mom, and I put coats on over shorts and walked to Whole Lotta Shakin' for brunch. In the dim light, the colored houses glowed. In the damp air, my hair curled.

Things felt normal. I felt better.

We sat at a table by the window. The guy with the dragonfly tattoo was behind the counter again. He waved me over. "Is that bald guy the famous William?" he whispered.

I wanted to giggle. The counter guy was way more bald than William was. But I whispered back, "That's him. And guess what? He called your cappuccino 'nectar of the gods.'"

"Whoa—get out! Talk like that could turn a fella's head. Yo! William!"

William looked up. The counter guy bowed. "Cappuccino's on me today! And I'll make it extra frothy."

William nodded and smiled as if counter guys always gave him extra-frothy cappuccinos for free. When I sat down, William asked, "Friend of yours?"

"I guess so. He can sing and dance, too."

We read the menu. Then I told what had happened with Laura, formerly known as yucky baby.

"You were going to close that tiny baby inside a cardboard carton?" Mom was horrified.

"It was perfectly safe," I said. "Probably. And anyway, we didn't. Annie changed her mind."

"I'm relieved to hear that," Mom said. "Why do you think she changed it?"

"I'm not sure exactly," I said. "But I've been thinking . . ."

The waitress came over. We ordered. I asked for salsa and chips with a sticky bun for dessert. William ordered oatmeal. Mom stuck with her healthy kick. She wanted a Greek salad and a mango lassi.

"What have you been thinking?" Mom asked after the waitress left.

"I can't explain very well," I said, "but I think maybe Annie used to be mad at the baby just for being a baby. And then she was holding the baby, and she was just about to stick her in the box . . . and close her up in the box . . . and, well, she thought about that. And she realized the baby is a person, too. And the baby has feelings. And then Annie wasn't so mad anymore."

I sounded stupid to myself. But William and Mom looked at me like I'd said something wise. And then they looked at each other.

Was it my imagination? Or was something going on?

What was it Mom wanted to talk to me about, anyway?

The counter guy came over with the free cappuccino.

"Very frothy indeed," said William. "Thank you."

"Do you want a duck joke or a San Francisco joke?" the counter guy asked.

"He tells jokes," I explained.

Mom said San Francisco.

The counter guy stood up straight. "What did Potrero Hill say to Mount Tam after the earthquake?"

Mom and William shrugged.

"We give up," I said.

"It wasn't my fault!" The counter guy waited for us to laugh. Mom and I smiled.

William said, "Perhaps duck was the better choice."

"Sorry." The counter guy spun around and did a dance step. "For duck, you have to come back."

The food came. A lassi is a yogurt shake. I watched Mom take a drink and wrinkle her nose. "You don't even like yogurt," I said. "And you ate that yogurt parfait the other day, too. What is it with all this healthy stuff?"

Mom doesn't turn jelly red when she's embarrassed. She turns more like lemonade pink. That's what happened now. She turned lemonade pink. And she looked up at William.

Something definitely was going on. "Okay." I put the chip back in the salsa and folded my arms across my chest. "Spill it."

Mom took a deep breath. She sighed. She gave me a sympathy look. "*You* don't think babies are yucky, Holly. Do you?"

Chapter 20

"The fog must have made the cardboard soggy," Dr. X said. "When I got up this morning, it looked like this."

We were standing with Annie in Dr. X's backyard. All that was left of the mysterious silver something was a sagging heap of foil, tin cans, and Christmas lights.

"Are you very sad about it?" Annie asked.

"I have time to build a new one," he said, "before Holly's baby comes."

"Oh, *no.*" I shook my head. "Not on my baby you don't. My baby won't be yucky in the first place."

"Yes it will," said Annie. "All babies start yucky. Even us. But somebody loved us anyway. So we have to love the new ones. That's how Grandmother explained it."

After brunch, my family had walked a block to a baby store. Babies these days have it made! There is so much cool stuff you can buy for them! I probably will give up chocolate and spend all my allowance on mobiles.

At the store, William picked out a baby blanket for Laura's bassinet. It had tiny pink cats on it. On the card, he wrote, "Sorry for the inconvenience," and he signed, "Boo Cat."

As soon as we got home, I had called Annie and Dr. X to tell them our news.

Dr. X was excited because he wanted to experiment on my new baby.

Annie was excited, too. "That makes us practically sisters!" she said.

I didn't see her logic. But it was a friendly thought.

On the phone, Dr. X told me something else. "I don't have a crush on Annie anymore. She lacks scientific curiosity."

"Good!" I said. "Then you can be friends."

We arranged to meet out here by what was left of the machine. We were planning to take it apart. We would save the lights and the fan and the twisty ties. We would recycle the cans, the cardboard, and the foil.

"Let's get started," said Dr. X. He kicked the de-yucka-ma-box; the sad soggy thing slumped over; a voice cried out from underneath: "Mrrrr-eee-ow!"

"Not again!" Annie said, but her words were almost drowned in a total chorus of unhappy meows. Then out from under the sagging heap poked two very familiar cat noses and a bunch of very familiar cat paws.

"Who let the cats out?" I asked.

"And why would they come here?" Dr. X asked.

"They sure seem to like the machine," Annie said.

"Lift it up slowly so we can catch them," I said.

Dr. X tilted the collapsed machine. Annie and I were ready to pounce. I expected four cats running in all directions. But instead there were three cats—Boo, Max, and George—and they didn't run. They walked. They sniffed the air. They side-rubbed our legs. They side-rubbed what was left of the machine.

"Why are they doing that?" Annie asked.

"I don't know. They act hungry." I remembered Max Cat the first day he ran into Dr. X's yard. Same thing. Was it the machine? What? I looked down at it. Foil. Cardboard. Lights. Cans. Cans.

"Dr. X," I said. "Did any of those cans used to be cat-food cans?"

Dr. X shook his head. "Of course not. All I've got is Copernicus."

So that wasn't it. Unless . . . "What about tuna? Were any of them tuna cans?"

"Heck, yeah," said Dr. X. "Tuna is Jim's favorite lunch."

"But I don't smell tuna," said Annie.

"Doesn't matter," I said. "Once a tuna can, always a tuna can—if you're a cat."

Chapter 21

"Do we have to eat healthy from now on?" I whined.

Mom smiled. "Get used to it."

Mom, William, and I were having dinner in our new pink house. It was the first dinner we'd eaten there. William made tofu enchiladas. Mom made a green salad. William lit candles. We sat at the dining room table. It was cozy.

"We have news," Mom said.

"Oh, no," I said. "Is it twins?"

Mom laughed. "I don't think so," she said. "This is a different kind of news. About the cats. You wondered how they were getting out?"

"Yeah?"

"There's a window in the basement," she said. "It's at ground level, and it was open just a crack."

"It's amazing a cat could squeeze through," said William, "especially George."

I thought of the incredible shrinking-cat trick. "Cats are amazing creatures," I said.

"True enough," said Mom.

"I hear you told the neighbors our other news," William said. "About the baby. How did they take it?"

"Mrs. Cohen said *mazel tov*," I said. "Alan said he hopes everything will be all right. Jim asked if he could be godfather. He knows how. He saw the movie *and* the sequel."

Mom and William laughed.

"I'll be happy so long as nobody puts this baby in a de-yucka-ma-box," Mom said.

I shrugged. "Dr. X is a junior genius. But I don't think his machine worked."

"I wouldn't be so sure," said William. "In the words of the bard, 'There are more things in heaven and earth, Horatio, Than are dreamt of in your philosophy.'"

"Who's Horatio?" I asked. "And what's a bard?"

"Horatio was Hamlet's best friend, the poor fellow. And a bard is a poet. When you say *the* bard, you mean Shakespeare," William explained.

"Other people can quote Shakespeare, too, you know." I faked a snotty accent: "'Some are born brave, some achieve bravery, and others have bravery thrust upon them.'"

"Where did you hear that?" William asked. "It's not 'bravery.' It's 'greatness.' And it's not Shakespeare; it's Winston Churchill. One of the wartime speeches."

"I think you're wrong," said Mom.

After dinner, we looked it up. It was Shakespeare—point for Mom. It was "greatness"—point for William.

I got into bed. Boo was hogging my pillow. Max was waiting by the door to escape. George had disappeared under the bed.

But where was Wilbur? I sat up and looked at my dresser. The sock drawer was closed. Maybe he had taken my suggestion. Maybe he was munching my old homework or William's ties.

But at that moment he sidled in. There was something in his mouth. I got scared. It wasn't a mouse, was it? I know some cats bring dead mice to their owners. It's supposed to be a gift. I didn't want that kind of gift.

Wilbur leaped onto my bed and curled up on my feet as usual. I sat up to see what he was chewing on.

Uh-oh. It looked like Wilbur would be sending a gift and a card to Laura, too. He was happily gnawing her pink Binky. I let him keep it. Even if I shook off the cat spit, I didn't think Annie would ever give it back to Laura.

Mom came in. She gave me a kiss.

"Every night I dream of boxes," she said. "I

guess it's moving. You put your life in a box; you take it back out. I wonder what the box does to it in the process."

"And now there's the baby coming, too," I said. "More changes."

"How do you feel about that?" Mom asked.

"Maybe it won't be so bad. I'm more of a slob than Annie. I don't mind yucky so much."

Mom laughed. "Did you know there's a Shakespeare quote about yucky, too?"

"You're kidding," I said. "What?"

Mom patted her belly. In the dark I could just see her smile. "He said, and I quote, 'Yucky is in the eye of the beholder.'"